Jerry's Trousers

For young Weston – a token of our hilarious adventures — Boz

For Robert — D.M.

First published 1998 by Macmillan Children's Books
This edition published 1998 by Macmillan Children's Books
a division of Macmillan Publishers Limited
20 New Wharf Road, London N1 9RR
Basingstoke and Oxford
Associated companies throughout the world
www.panmacmillan.com

ISBN 0 333 68359 5

Text copyright © Nigel Boswall 1998
Illustrations copyright © David Melling 1998

3 5 7 9 8 6 4

A CIP catalogue record for this book
is available from the British Library.

Printed in China

Jerry's Trousers

Nigel Boswall and David Melling

MACMILLAN CHILDREN'S BOOKS

"Decisions, decisions," sighed Jerry, "life is full of decisions. Now, just which trousers shall I take on my trip to England?"

At last, the choice was made.

A pair for travelling,

a pair for flying kites,

a pair for boating,

a pair for the park,

and finally a pair for parties.

His friend Billy met Jerry at the airport.
"How was your flight, Jerry?" asked Billy.
"Well," replied Jerry, "when you've travelled
as much as I have, flying in a plane is nothing."

Just then a car sped by, right through a large puddle. Billy jumped back just in time. But Jerry was soaked.

"Don't worry. These things happen, even to the best travellers," said Billy sympathetically.

"Perfect day for flying a kite," said Billy,
as he tugged on the string.

"Oh, no – you don't want to do it like
that!" cried Jerry. "Here, watch me."

Jerry started to run, the kite flying up
behind him. It started to twist and dive,
and ended up in the middle of a thick
clump of bushes.

Jerry pulled and pulled on the string, but the kite was well and truly stuck.

He strode into the bushes,

he crawled under the brambles,

he kicked at the branches.

"Aha!" exclaimed Jerry. "Got it!"
And then he looked down at his trousers.
"Don't worry. These things happen,
even to the best kite fliers," said Billy kindly.

"Beautiful day to be on the lake," said Billy,
rowing carefully past a family of ducks.

"Yes, beautiful," agreed Jerry. "But you
should take longer strokes. Here, let me!"

The boat rocked dangerously from side
to side as Jerry changed seats with Billy.

The little boat picked up speed.
"Slow down, Jerry . . . Jerry, please!"
begged Billy. But too late. BANG!
Jerry crashed into another boat.

Jerry hung his shrinking trousers on a radiator.
"Don't worry. These things happen, even to
the best sailors," said Billy gently.

"Wonderful day to be in the park," said Billy,
standing shakily on his rollerblades.

"Make way! Make way!" Jerry shouted
as he whizzed along the path.
Several passers-by stopped to watch.
Some even clapped.

Jerry leaped into the air, waving back to
the crowd. But landing was not so easy.
There was a loud tearing sound.

Jerry tried to repair his trousers.
"Don't worry. These things happen,
even to the best skaters," said Billy quietly.

"Splendid day for a party," said Billy
as he introduced Jerry to his friends.

"I *must* tell you what I've been up to!"
said Jerry. He showed them

how to fly a kite,

how to row a boat,

how to rollerblade.

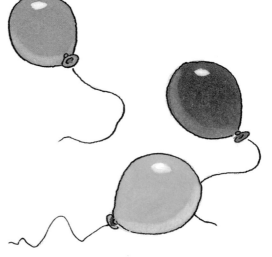

Billy came into the room carrying
a surprise cake for his friend.
But Jerry was far too busy to notice.

Cake flew everywhere.

Billy helped Jerry up.

"Don't worry. These things happen, even at the best parties," said Billy patiently.

Jerry looked at his trousers laid out on the bed.
"How can I wear a single pair of them again?"
he sighed.

Billy walked up and down, deep in thought.
Suddenly, he stopped.

"I think," he said excitedly, "you might be able
to wear *all* of them again."

"That's brilliant!" Jerry exclaimed, admiring
his new trousers. "I've been so silly and now
you've been so clever."

Only the shrunken pair was left.

"Look after your new trousers!" called Jerry.
"And you look after yours!" Billy called back.
"Don't worry. I won't let anything happen to my best trousers," replied Jerry. "After all, they were made for me by my best friend!"